SCARY HARRY

BY LISA TRUMBAUER
ILLUSTRATED BY SUSAN LEXA

CHAPTERS

Harcourt
Orlando Boston Dallas Chicago San Diego

Visit *The Learning Site!*
www.harcourtschool.com

Scary Harry

"Are you looking through that thing again?"

Harry turned his head from the telescope to glare at his older brother. Robert always thought what Harry did was not cool.

Harry thought differently. He knew that studying space was the coolest thing on the planet. Even if it wasn't really *on* the planet.

"Searching for comets is great," Harry told Robert over his shoulder.

Robert was munching a hot dog. They had eaten dinner only a few hours ago, but that didn't stop Robert from eating again.

Robert shrugged. "I don't see the point in looking at something that's so far away."

Harry shook his head and continued to gaze through his telescope. The planets were amazing and full of mystery. What lay beyond the planets was even more exciting.

As he finished his hot dog, Robert asked, "So do you ever actually see comets with this thing?"

"Of course," said Harry.

"Well, just to bring you back to Earth, we're getting new neighbors tomorrow. See you later."

Harry turned back to his telescope as Robert left the room. He searched the dark sky for any sign of movement. Harry was looking for a comet. Some people thought a comet was a shooting star. Actually, it was a ball of ice and rock going through space. It traveled in an orbit through the solar system, just like the planets. It had an orbit around the sun, too.

Harry wanted to be the first person to discover a new comet. He wanted that more than anything.

Tonight was not the night. The night sky was studded with stars, but it was very still. Harry stood watching for a while. Then he laid down on his bed. He looked up at the ceiling. Even his ceiling had a pattern of stars. His parents had let him paint stars on it with glow-in-the-dark paint. When Harry turned out the lights, the stars glowed.

Harry thought about the new neighbors. He wondered if there would be any kids. Not that it mattered. Most kids thought Harry's interest in space was strange.

Sure, other kids liked to imagine weird creatures visiting Earth from other planets. To Harry, that was just make-believe. Harry took studying space seriously. If kids said they thought aliens lived on Jupiter, Harry told them that couldn't be true.

So kids thought Harry was a little weird. Instead of playing soccer, like they did, Harry would map out the stars and identify constellations. Instead of reading scary stories, Harry enjoyed his collection of nonfiction space books.

"Maybe I *am* weird," Harry mumbled to himself as he got ready for bed.

Something Mysterious

Harry woke up Saturday feeling much better. Maybe today he'd discover that comet! And, of course, today was the day the new neighbors were moving in.

First, Harry looked out his window. A large moving van was already on the street. Then he watched as big, brown boxes and furniture were unloaded and carried inside the house next door. He didn't see any kids or bikes or toys.

Harry got dressed, grabbed a banana from the kitchen, and raced outside. He sat on the front step and watched the action.

So far, nothing exciting had happened. Harry saw a blue sofa, a washing machine, a rocking chair, a mattress wrapped in plastic, and lots of big, brown boxes.

Suddenly, a very large object was taken from the truck. It was covered with a large blanket. Three metal feet were poking from the bottom. What looked like one large, thick arm stuck out on the side.

What could the mysterious object be? A million thoughts raced through Harry's mind. Suddenly, a teenage girl came flying out of the house. "Be careful with that!" she exclaimed. "Put that down, please. It's delicate."

Then she saw Harry. "Hi!" she said.

"Hi," Harry said shyly.

"I'm Sera. Could you help me with something?"

"Sure!" Harry said, standing up. He threw away his banana peel and strolled over.

"I'm scared the movers will damage my equipment," she said. "Could you help me carry it into the house?"

Robert carried things better than Harry. Robert was asleep, though. The last time Harry woke Robert up, Robert threw a shoe at him.

"Sure, I'll help," Harry said. "My name is Harry."

"Pleased to meet you, Harry," Sera said. Harry thought Sera was pretty. She had long, dark hair and big, brown eyes. She wore glasses, just like Harry.

"Hold it gently," Sera instructed. She wrapped her arms around the top. Harry wrapped his hands around the bottom.

"I'm going to count to three," Sera said. "Then we'll lift it together. Okay?"

"Sure," Harry said. He fastened his arms more securely around the three legs.

"One, two, three!" As Sera lifted, Harry lifted. It wasn't easy. The three legs almost tripped Harry as he walked.

Finally, they made it into the house. Harry and Sera carefully set the device down. Harry was dying to know what it was.

“Thanks!” Sera said. “That was a big help.”

Harry had to ask. “So, um, what is it?”

Sera smiled. “You probably wouldn’t be interested. Most people aren’t.”

“I am,” Harry said hopefully.

Sera studied him for a moment. “Maybe you are,” she said. “Help me take the blanket off.”

Harry carefully helped Sera uncover the mystery device. Harry held his breath.

“Oh!” he said. “A telescope!”

Sera's telescope was much bigger than Harry's. It looked complicated.

"I want to be an astronomer someday," Sera told him. "That means I have to practice using the telescope to study stars."

"I know," Harry said. "I have a telescope, too."

"Really?" Sera said.

"Sure. I'm looking for a comet."

"Are you?" Sera asked. "I know where you can see one tonight."

Harry's jaw dropped. A real comet!

"Are you joking?" Harry asked, too surprised to say any more.

"I never joke about outer space," Sera said. "Would you like to come with me and my family to watch for it? We're going to Walnut Hill later tonight."

Harry couldn't believe it. His new neighbor had a telescope. His new neighbor liked outer space. His new neighbor was going to look at comets!

That night, Harry went to Walnut Hill with his new neighbors. Harry and Sera and her parents weren't the only people there. Many people had turned out to see the comet.

"How did all these people know about the comet?" Harry asked.

"There is a special comet website," Sera told him. "I'll give you the address later."

Harry set up his telescope beside Sera's. Together, they pointed their telescopes toward the sky.

"Hey, Scary Harry!" came a voice.

It was Harry's brother, Robert, … and their parents!

"Mom and Dad didn't want to miss the fun," Robert said. "I thought I'd come, too."

Suddenly, everyone on Walnut Hill became very excited.

Harry looked through his telescope. It was a comet!

"It looks like a big mustache!" Harry laughed.

"Let's call it Mustache Comet," said Sera.

Harry smiled. Maybe someday Sera and he would find a new comet together.